For Pat and Sheila

THE TIME IT TOOK TOM

Nick Sharratt
Stephen Tucker

SCHOLASTIC
PRESS

With thanks to
David Fickling, Ness Wood
and John Peacock

Scholastic Children's Books,
Commonwealth House, 1-19 New Oxford Street,
London WC1A 1NU, UK
a division of Scholastic Ltd

London ~ New York ~ Toronto ~ Sydney ~ Auckland

First published by Scholastic Ltd, 1998

ISBN 0 590 54323 7 (hardback)
ISBN 0 590 11427 1 (paperback)

Printed in China

Tom found the red paint.

It took him three seconds
to decide what to
do with it.

One.

Two.

Three.

It took him (*oof!*) three (*humpf!*) minutes to get the (*grrrrrrrrrrrr!*) lid off the tin!

It took him three hours to paint the front room.

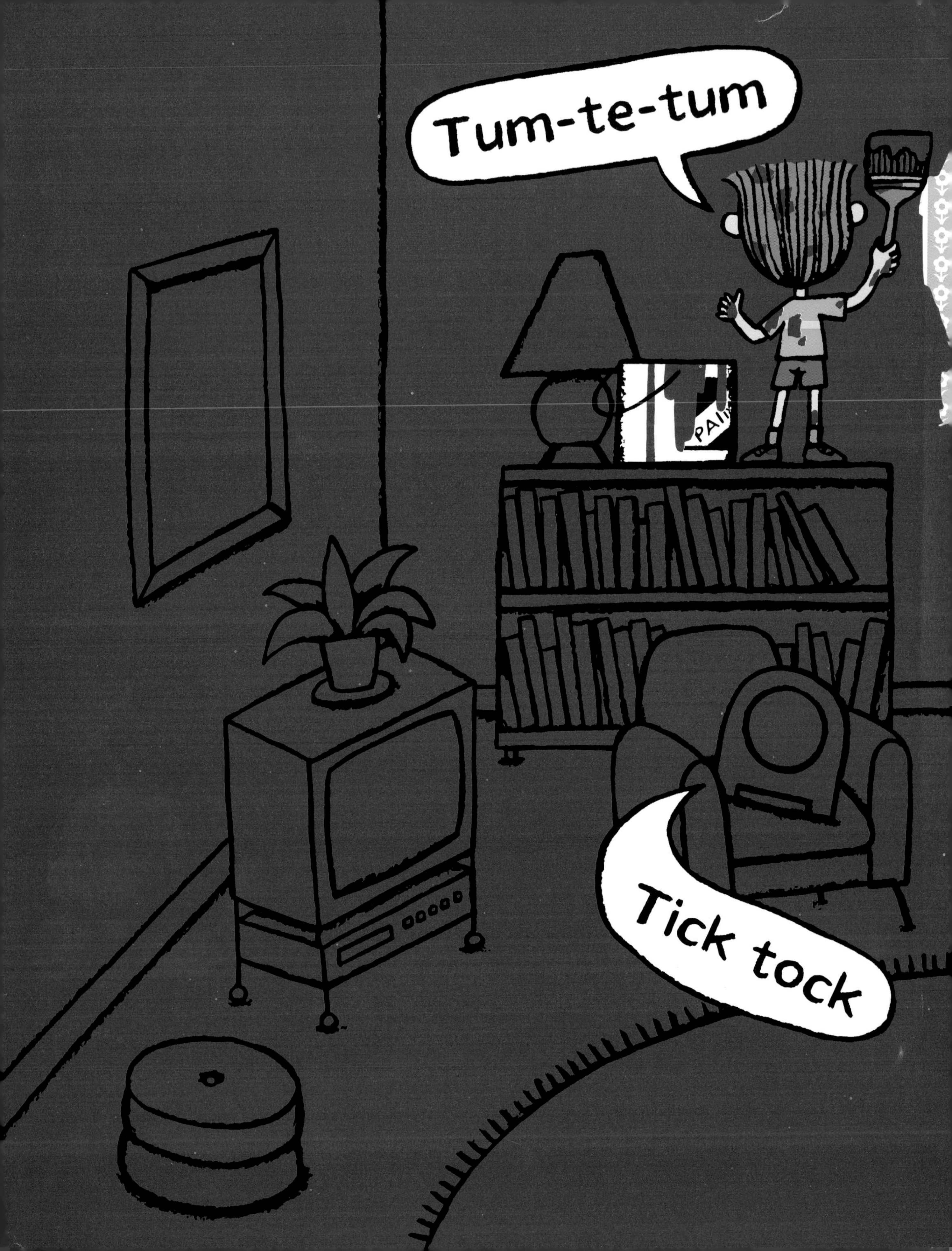
Tum-te-tum
Tick tock
PAI

Three hours.

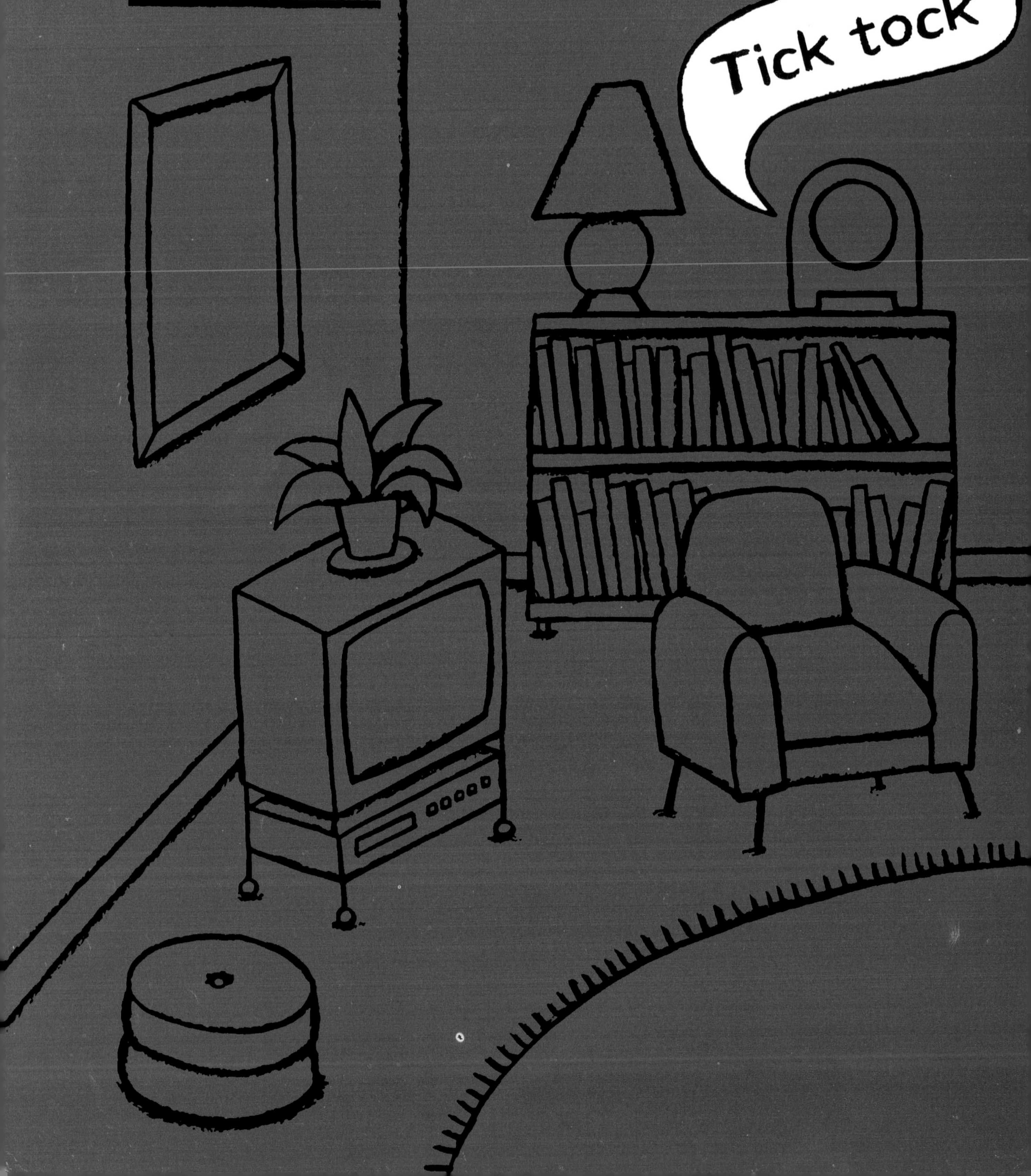

Tom's mum came in.
It took her *ten*
         nine
         eight
         seven
         six
         five
         four
         three
         two
         one

seconds to **explode!**

It took three weeks.

And this is how we did it.

 We had to get a skip

For the ruined bits of furniture.

 We stripped off all the wallpaper,

And went off to the store, *Brrm*

 To buy some tins of paint

(There were loads of different colours)

And pick a paper that we liked

 From all the ones we saw.

We sandpapered the woodwork

 And we painted it with undercoat.

We started putting gloss paint

On the window frame [ ] and door.

And that's when Mum decided

That she didn't like the colour,

 So we stopped what we were doing

And we went back to the store.

Here's a list of what we painted:

The window and the skirting board

The bookcase and the table

And the sideboard  and the door.

 And this time Mum was happy

And I was even happier

Because I really didn't feel

 Like painting any more!

 Mum hung the paper (by herself!)

 Men came and laid the carpet

And after that we had to make

A last trip to the store . . .  Brrm

For a sofa 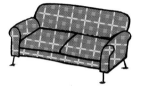 and an armchair

 And a telly and a video

Some curtains for the window,

And a new rug for the floor.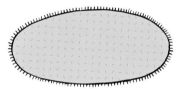

We also bought a little tree

(But that was for the garden)

And a footstool and a fruitbowl

And a nice plant in a pot,

Cushions,   lamps, a mirror,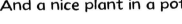

Some pictures of the countryside,

A clock, a vase,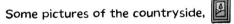

A photoframe,

And that's about the lot!

One year went by.

Two year.

went by.

Three   years went by.

Tom found the blue paint.